A Charlie Brown Christmas™

A Charlie Brown
CHRISTMAS™

BY CHARLES M. SCHULZ

RP|KIDS

PHILADELPHIA • LONDON

Printed in China

*This book may not be reproduced in whole or in part,
in any form or by any means, electronic or mechanical,
including photocopying, recording, or by any information
storage and retrieval system now known or hereafter
invented, without written permission from the publisher.*

9 8 7 6 5 4 3 2 1
Digit on the right indicates the number of this printing

Library of Congress Control Number: 2007942767

Adapted by Megan E. Bryant
Art Adapted by Tom Brannon
Cover and interior design by Frances J. Soo Ping Chow
Edited by Kelli Chipponeri
Typography: Abadi, Bembo, and Chuck

This special edition was printed for Kohl's Department
Stores, Inc. (for distribution on behalf of Kohl's Cares,
LLC, its wholly owned subsidiary)
Published by Running Press Kids
An Imprint of Running Press Book Publishers
A Member of the Perseus Books Group
2300 Chestnut Street
Philadelphia, PA 19103-4371

Kohl's
ISBN 978-0-7624-5145-6
123386
First Edition Printed 04/13–09/13

Visit us on the web!
www.runningpress.com
www.Snoopy.com
www.Kohls.com/Cares

CHRISTMASTIME was here—the time when snowflakes fell softly and the sounds of carols rang through the air. It was the time filled with happiness. And for children everywhere, it was their favorite time of year.

But one little boy wasn't feeling very excited about Christmas.

"I just don't understand Christmas," Charlie Brown said, as a light snow began to fall. "I might be getting presents, sending Christmas cards, and decorating trees, but I'm still not happy. I always end up feeling depressed."

"You're the only person I know who can take a wonderful season like Christmas and turn it into a problem," Linus replied. "Lucy's right. Of all the Charlie Browns in the world, you're the Charlie Browniest."

At the local skating pond, the boys found their friends playing a round of crack-the-whip. Snoopy grabbed Linus's blanket to drag him onto the ice—but he caught Charlie Brown in it, and sent him flying into a snow bank!

Charlie Brown wasn't surprised. Things like that *always* happened to him. And the holiday season, when he didn't get cards and even his own dog ignored him, only made it more obvious. He needed someone to talk to.

Lucy dashed over to her psychiatry booth to meet

Charlie Brown. "May I help you?" she asked.

"I am in sad shape," Charlie Brown replied with a

sigh. "My trouble is Christmas. I just don't understand it.

Instead of feeling happy, I feel sort of let down."

Lucy knew just how to fix Charlie Brown's problem.
"You need to get involved in a Christmas project," she
declared. "How would you like to be the director of our
Christmas play?"

"Me? But I don't know anything about directing a
Christmas play," Charlie Brown fretted.

"Don't worry. I'll be there to help you," Lucy said.
"I'll meet you at the auditorium!"

Just then Snoopy walked past, carrying a box filled with decorations. Charlie Brown followed Snoopy back to his doghouse.

"What's going on here?" Charlie Brown asked. Snoopy handed him a flyer, and Charlie Brown read, "'Find the true meaning of Christmas. Win money, money, money at the spectacular, super-colossal lights and display contest!' Oh, no. My own dog has gone commercial. I can't stand it!" Charlie Brown threw the flyer on the ground.

On his way to the auditorium, he ran into his sister, Sally.

"I've been looking for you, big brother," she said sweetly. "Will you please write a letter to Santa Claus for me?"

Sally knew exactly what she wanted, but her list was so long. She decided it would be easier to ask for money. "How about tens and twenties?" she suggested.

"Tens and twenties? Oh, even my baby sister!" Charlie Brown groaned. Surely Christmas was about more than money and presents!

In the auditorium, the whole Peanuts gang danced to a jazzy tune that Schroeder played on his piano.

Charlie Brown walked onto the stage. "Let's get right down to work," he said. "It's important that you pay strict attention to the director. Am I right? I said, am I right?"

But no one paid any attention to Charlie Brown. They had started dancing again!

"Stop the music!" Charlie Brown yelled. "We're going to do this play and we're going to do it right. Lucy, pass out those scripts and costumes."

One by one, the kids found out their roles in the play. Frieda would play the innkeeper's wife. Pig Pen would play the innkeeper. Shermy would play the shepherd. And Snoopy would play all the animals in the script—and even some that weren't!

"Let's rehearse the scene at the inn," directed Charlie Brown. "Let's take it from the top! Places! ACTION!"

But once more, the kids started dancing and fooling around. Charlie Brown rolled his eyes. "Good grief!"

"That does it!" Charlie Brown exclaimed. "If we're ever going to get this play off the ground, we've got to have some cooperation!"

"Let's face it," replied Lucy. "We all know that Christmas is a big commercial racket."

"Well, this is one play that's not going to be commercial!" Charlie Brown insisted. "We need the proper mood. We need a Christmas tree!"

Lucy nodded excitedly. "A great, big, shiny aluminum Christmas tree! That's it, Charlie Brown! You get the tree. I'll handle this crowd."

"Okay. I'll take Linus with me. The rest of you—practice your lines," Charlie Brown said firmly.

"Get the biggest aluminum tree you can find, Charlie Brown!" called Lucy.

"Yeah. Do something right for a change, Charlie Brown," added Peppermint Patty as the boys walked into the cold winter night.

They followed a set of gleaming spotlights to a Christmas tree lot. It was filled with shiny metal trees, polka-dotted trees, and trees in every color of the rainbow.

Clank. Clank. Clank. Linus knocked on one of the metal trees. "Gee, do they still make wooden Christmas trees?" asked Linus. He didn't see anything like that in the Christmas tree lot.

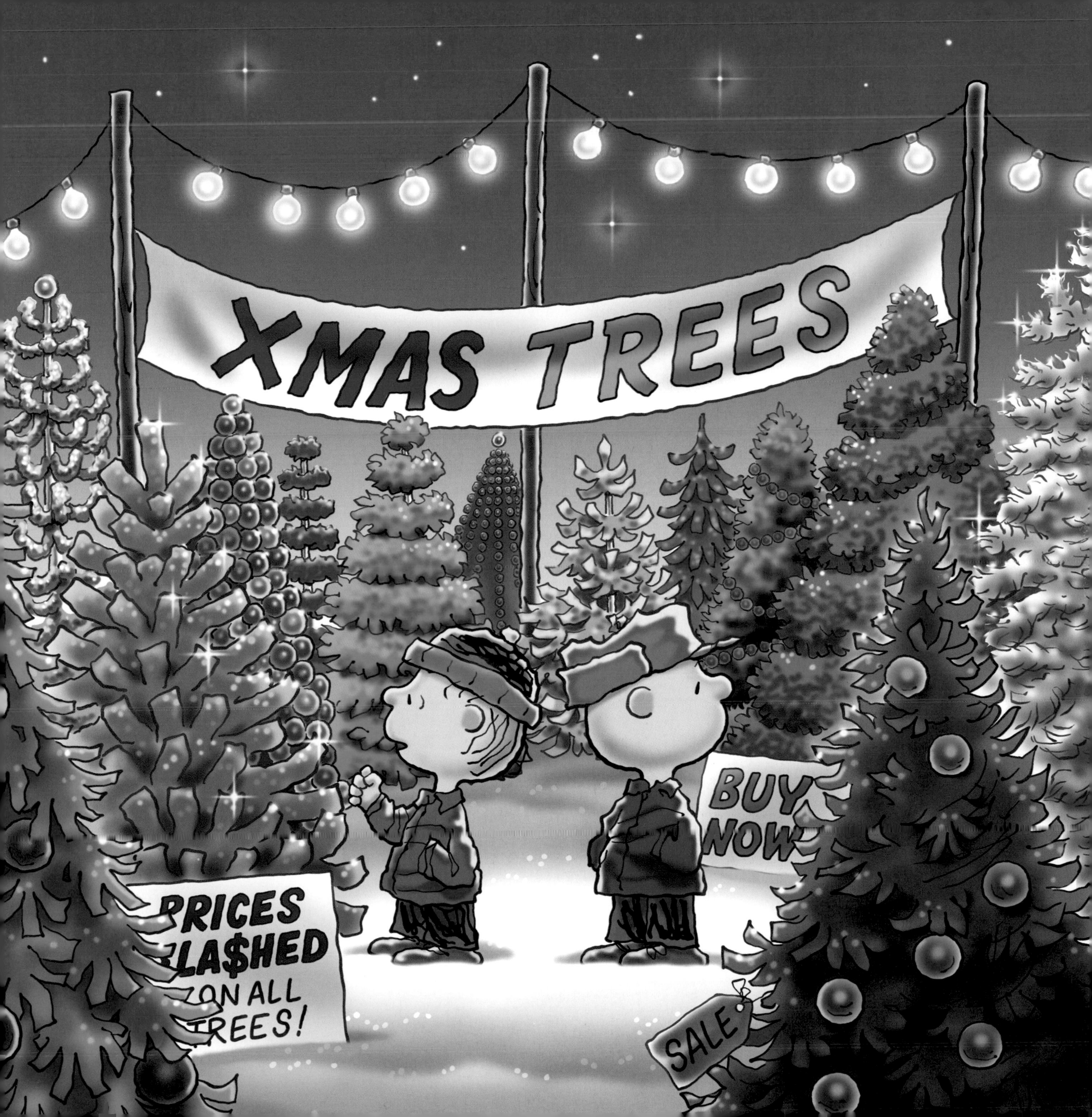
XMAS TREES
BUY NOW
PRICES SLA$HED ON ALL TREES!
SALE

Then Charlie Brown spotted a small, scraggly pine tree. It had a wooden trunk and soft green needles. "This little green one here seems to need a good home!" he said excitedly.

"I don't know, Charlie Brown," Linus said. "Remember what Lucy said? This doesn't seem to fit the modern spirit."

"I don't care," Charlie Brown insisted. "We'll decorate it and it will be just right for our play. Besides, I think it needs me."

Soon Charlie Brown and Linus walked onto the stage.

"We're back!" Charlie Brown announced as he set the tree on top of Schroeder's piano.

When the kids rushed over to see the tree, their mouths dropped in shock. The scraggly little tree was *not* what they had expected.

"You were supposed to get a good tree. Can't you even tell a good tree from a poor tree?" Lucy asked.

"You're hopeless, Charlie Brown!" added Peppermint Patty.

Charlie Brown sighed. "I shouldn't have picked this little tree. Everything I do turns into a disaster. I guess I really don't know what Christmas is all about. Isn't there *anyone* who knows what Christmas is all about?" he exclaimed.

"Sure, Charlie Brown," replied Linus. "I can tell you what Christmas is all about."

Linus crossed to the center of the stage. The lights dimmed, and a spotlight shone down on him.

"And there were shepherds in the field, keeping watch over their flock by night. The angel came and said, 'Fear not, for behold, I bring you tidings of great joy, which will be to all people. For unto you is born this day a savior, which is Christ the Lord. Ye shall find the babe wrapped in swaddling clothes lying in a manger.' And suddenly there was with the angel a multitude of the heavenly host, praising God and saying, 'Glory to God in the highest, and on Earth peace, goodwill toward men.'"

Everyone was silent when Linus finished. "That's what Christmas is all about, Charlie Brown," he finally said.

Charlie Brown picked up the tree and walked outside.

He stared up at the night sky. "Linus is right," he said. "I

won't let all this commercialism ruin my Christmas. I'll take

this little tree home and decorate it and I'll show them it

really will work in our play."

When he passed Snoopy's doghouse, Charlie Brown pulled a shiny red ornament off the doghouse and proudly hung it on the tree.

But the tiny tree buckled under the weight of the ornament. A look of horror crossed Charlie Brown's face. "I've killed it! Oh, everything I touch gets ruined!" His head hung in defeat, Charlie Brown sadly walked away.

Then the rest of the Peanuts gang arrived.

"I never thought it was such a bad little tree," Linus said. He straightened the tree's bent trunk and wrapped his blanket around its base. "It's not bad at all, really. It just needs a little love."

Without speaking, the other kids took the lights and ornaments off Snoopy's doghouse and used them to decorate. Before their very eyes it transformed into a beautiful Christmas tree!

Charlie Brown walked up to the group—and barely recognized the tree. "What's going on here?" he exclaimed.

"Merry Christmas, Charlie Brown!" the kids exclaimed. And together, gathered around that beautiful Christmas tree, they all began to sing:

Hark, the herald angels sing,   *Joyful, all ye nations, rise!*
Glory to the newborn King!   *Join the triumph of the skies!*
Peace on Earth and mercy mild   *With angelic host proclaim:*
God and sinner reconciled.   *Christ is born in Bethlehem.*

Hark, the herald angels sing,
Glory to the newborn King.